Kennedy +
You are loved!
- Mat

I Think of You

Kennedy + Kamden

MARIE WHITE

ZAMIZ PRESS

DEDICATION

To Joshua, Isabelle, Rachel, Branson, Ryder, Ava, Braxton, Landon, Aiden, Ariella, Everbelle, Ryland and Brody.
To every child who can't be with those they love.
You are never forgotten.

This book is for

Kennedy + Kam

From

Grandma

W hen the sky is bright blue and butterflies come out to play, I wonder if you're playing in the grass and I think of you.

W hen the wind sweeps across the trees and it gets a little cold, I wonder if you have a coat to keep you warm and I think of you.

W hen it's cold outside and Christmas is very near, I wonder if Santa will bring what's on your list and I think of you.

W hen spring is just beginning and flowers are in bloom, I stop to smell the flowers and I think of you.

W hen the rain is coming down and clouds are in the sky, I wonder if you're warm and dry and I think of you.

When the weather's hot and the sun is shining down, I wonder if you have a cold drink and I think of you.

When I drive past the park and see children just like you, I wonder if you're having fun and I think of you.

W hen it's your birthday, with cake and ice cream, I say a prayer that your day is great and I think of you.

W hen you're tying your shoes or brushing your hair, even though I'm not there, I think of you.

When you're scared or alone and don't know what to do, know that I'm praying when I think of you.

When it's been a bad day and your heart is feeling blue, know that I'll always love you and I think of you.

W hen it's daytime and when it's night...

No matter where you are, know that I'll always love you and I think of you.

Even when you can't see me, I'm always praying for God to keep you safe and I think of you.

Did you like the dog in the story? Get the matching stuffed animal called the "Aurora World Mini Flopsie Scotty Dog" at http://amzn.to/2j90LqD.

ABOUT THE AUTHOR

Marie White is the award-winning, bestselling author of seven books, including *Strength for Parents of Missing Children: Surviving Divorce, Abduction, Runaways and Foster Care.* She began writing when her toddler was abducted.

She is a non-denominational Christian missionary, traveler and YouTube host.

You can connect with Marie at www.MarieWhiteAuthor.com.

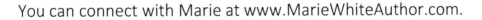

Made in the USA
San Bernardino, CA
13 March 2018